First U.S. edition 2015

Library of Congress Catalog Card Number 2014939366

ISBN 978-0-7636-7607-0

15 16 17 18 19 20 SFP 10 9 8 7 6 5 4 3 2 1

Printed in Shenzhen, Guangdong, China

This book was typeset in Tweaked Ammy's Handwriting.
The illustrations were created digitally.

Nosy Crow
An imprint of
Candlewick Press
99 Dover Street
Somerville, Massachusetts 02144

www.nosycrow.com
www.candlewick.com

FOR ALL OUR SMALLER SELVES
S. P.

FOR MUM AND DAD, WITH LOVE
A. P.

MOUSE'S FIRST NIGHT AT
MOONLIGHT SCHOOL

SIMON PUTTOCK
illustrated by ALI PYE

nosy crow
An imprint of Candlewick Press

The night bell was about to ring at
Miss Moon's Moonlight School,

and Bat

and Cat

and Owl were all on their way.

But somebody was missing, and
that somebody was Mouse.

It was Mouse's first night at school, and she was feeling shy. So she had come in extra early and hidden behind a curtain.

"Has anyone seen Mouse?"
asked Miss Moon.

Owl put up his wing.

"Yes, Owl?"
asked Miss Moon.

"I have not seen
Mouse," said Owl.

Cat put up her paw.
"Sadly, I have not seen
Mouse, either," she said.

"Bat," asked Miss Moon,
"have you seen Mouse?"

"No, Miss Moon," said Bat.
"I have never seen Mouse, ever!"

"How mysterious,"
said Miss Moon.
"Mouse, dear,
are you here?"

Now, Mouse's mother had said to Mouse, "Be sure to behave," so . . .

"I am here," said Mouse in a very small voice, a voice so small it could hardly be heard.

"Did somebody say something?" Miss Moon asked.

"I did!" called Mouse.
"And I am hiding because I am shy."

"But where are you?"
asked Miss Moon.

"I'm hiding behind the curtain!"

"Well then," said Miss Moon,
"why don't you come out so
that everyone can meet you?"

Now, Mouse's mother had said to Mouse,
"Be sure to behave," so Mouse crept
out from behind the curtain.

"That was great
hiding," said Bat.

"When I hide,"
said Owl, "parts of me
always stick out."

"Me too," said Cat,
"and I have to remember
not to purr."

"I like hiding,"
said Mouse.

"I have an idea,"
said Miss Moon . . .

"Let's play hide-and-seek
right now!
Then we can have our
midnight snacks."

Miss Moon closed
her eyes and counted:

"1, 2, 3, 4, 5, 6, 7, 8, 9, 10."

"Ready or not," she cried, "here I come!"

Miss Moon found Owl first.

A lot
of him was
sticking out.

Then Miss Moon
found Cat. She was
purring very loudly.

PURR PURR PURR PURR PURR

Miss Moon found Bat, too.
The fishbowl was easy
to see through!

But Miss Moon
could not find
Mouse.

"Mouse really **is** good at hiding,"
said Miss Moon.

"Let's all look for her together."

So they looked inside
the paint pots . . .

and they looked on top of cupboards,
and they looked under a pile of leaves.
But they couldn't find Mouse anywhere.

"Oh, dear," said Miss Moon.
"Mouse's mother will be upset
if we've lost her."

Then Miss Moon heard a tiny laugh. "That sounds like Mouse!" she said.

"Tee-hee," Mouse laughed again.
"You didn't find me!"

"That's true, dear," said Miss Moon,
"but now it's time for midnight snacks,
so do come out, and we can all
have something nice to eat."

Mouse crept out from her hiding place.
She had been hiding in Miss Moon's
hat-flowers all along!

"Good job, Mouse," said Miss Moon. "You **are** the best at hiding!"

Owl, Bat, and Cat agreed.

Mouse
was so pleased
that she forgot all
about being shy.

And she never
hid from
her friends
again . . .

unless, of course,
they were playing hide-and-seek!